Gori

Written by Jack Gabolinscy

Gorillas are apes.
They have a big head
with little ears and
little eyes.
Gorillas do not have a tail.

ear

3

Gorillas are very big.
They can be big like people.
Look at the arms and
the legs.
The arms are long.
The legs are short.

short legs

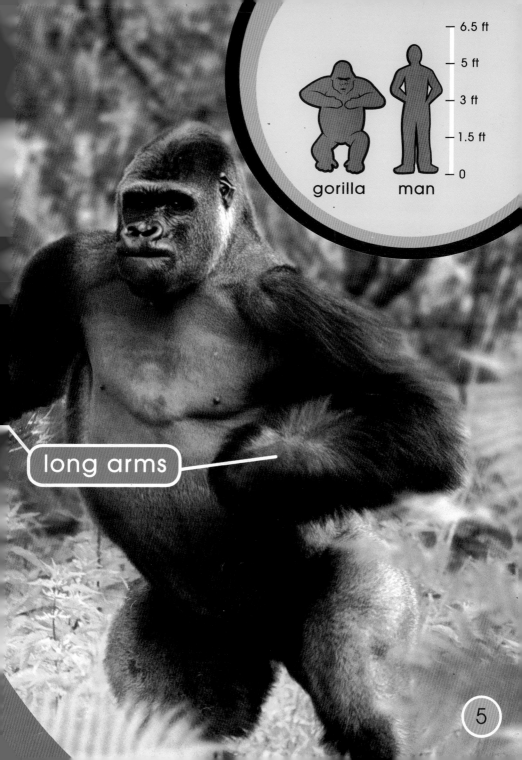

6.5 ft

5 ft

3 ft

1.5 ft

0

gorilla   man

long arms

5

Gorillas look for food
to eat in the day.
They like to sleep
in the day, too.

leaves

shoots

A gorilla will
make a nest at night.
Some gorillas make their nests
in the trees.
They can sleep in the nest.

nest

Some gorillas make their nests on the ground.

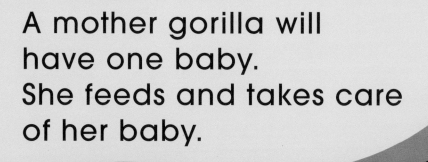

A mother gorilla will have one baby. She feeds and takes care of her baby.

baby gorilla

Key

where gorillas live

Gorillas live in the forest. They will stay away from people.

But people go into their forest.
They cut down the trees!
Where will the gorillas live?
Where will they get food
to eat?

Index

Guide Notes

Title: Gorillas
Stage: Early (3) – Blue

Genre: Nonfiction
Approach: Guided Reading
Processes: Thinking Critically, Exploring Language, Processing Information
Written and Visual Focus: Photographs (static images), Index, Labels, Caption, Graph, Map
Word Count: 132

THINKING CRITICALLY
(sample questions)
- Look at the front cover and the title. Ask the children what they know about gorillas.
- Look at the title and read it to the children.
- Focus the children's attention on the index. Ask: "What are you going to find out about in this book?"
- If you want to find out about a gorilla's legs, what page would you look on?
- If you want to find out about where gorillas live, what page would you look on?
- Look at pages 8 and 9. Why do you think the gorilla makes its nest in a tree?
- Look at pages 14 and 15. What do you think will happen to the gorillas if all the trees in the forest are cut down?
- How do you think a gorilla would hide from people?

EXPLORING LANGUAGE

Terminology
Title, cover, photographs, author, photographers

Vocabulary
Interest words: gorilla, forest, ape, nest
High-frequency words: day, eat, from, one, their
Positional words: in, down

Print Conventions
Capital letter for sentence beginnings, periods, comma, exclamation mark, question marks